THIS BOOK BELONGS TO:

Emma

Love-
Ms. Sherral

GOOD NIGHT, LITTLE ONE

BY STEVE BJÖRKMAN

WATERBROOK
PRESS

GOOD NIGHT, LITTLE ONE
Published by WaterBrook Press
5446 North Academy Boulevard, Suite 200
Colorado Springs, Colorado 80918
A division of Random House, Inc.

ISBN 1-57856-275-9

Text and illustrations copyright © 1999 by Steve Björkman

Printed in the United States of America
1999—First Edition

10 9 8 7 6 5 4 3 2 1

For Diane.
Your insight, inspiration,
and love are here in every page.
Thank you.

Good night, little ones in bed everywhere.

It's a night for big kisses and rumpling your hair

and telling you how much God knows you and cares.

Good night, little ones in bed everywhere.

Good night, little bunny, so snug in your bed;

There's a storm up above, but you're dry and well fed.

God has protected you, just as He said.

Good night, little bunny, so snug in your bed.

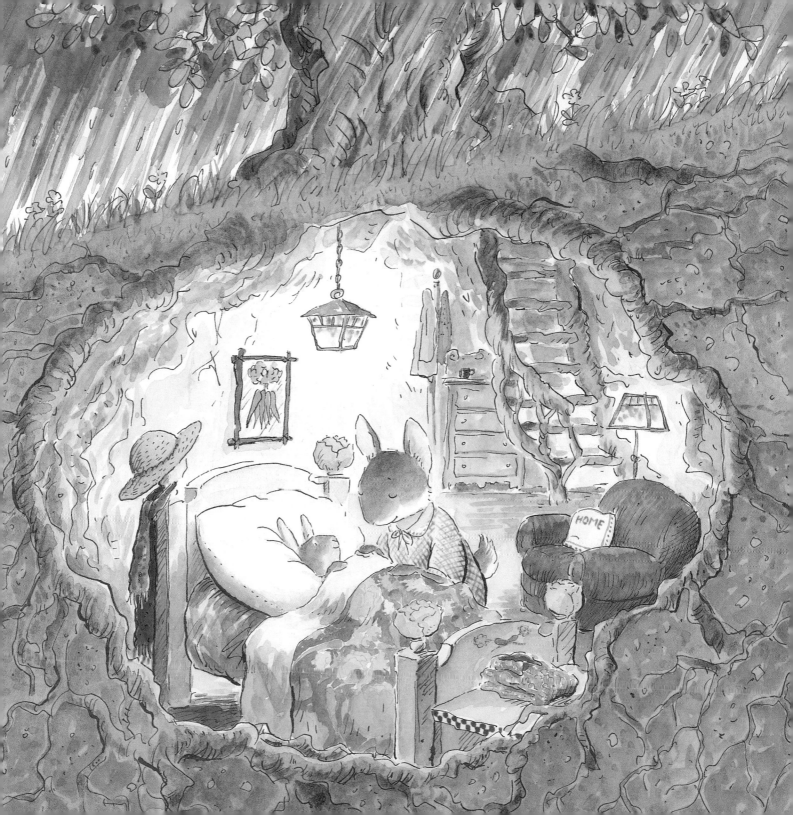

Good night, little sparrow; it's hard to be small.

You have little wings, and you're not very tall.

But God will defend you and come when you call.

Good night, little sparrow; it's okay to be small.

Good night, little skunk; you were a stinker today.

You did what was wrong and then got away.

But God always sees it when you disobey.

Good night, little skunk; you were a stinker today.

Good night, my raccoon; you've had quite a fright!

You wandered away and got lost in the night.

But God sent your dad with a very big light.

Good night, my raccoon; you've had quite a fright!

Good night, little bear; you're growing so strong.

You ate berries and honey and bugs all day long!

And God loves to give you a heart full of song.

Good night, little bear; you're growing so strong.

Good night, little rat, with your tail in a knot.

You're angry because you did wrong and got caught.

You need to say "sorry" and do what you ought.

God forgives little rats with their tails in a knot.

Good night, little squirrel; you are hungry, I know.

But God up above cares for you down below.

He'll provide what you need so you can grow.

Good night, little squirrel; you are hungry, I know.

Good night, little fox; you thought you were smart,

till the farmer caught you in an upside-down cart.

But God let you escape! Now you have a fresh start.

God still cares for foxes who think they are smart.

Good night, little weasel, with beady brown eyes.

You think no one likes you, and sometimes you cry.

But God loves you so, and I'm not surprised.

Good night, little weasel, with beady brown eyes.

Good night, little fawn, all speckled and brown.

You're safe in the grass, huddled there on the ground.

You can take a long nap; God is always around!

Good night, little fawn, all speckled and brown.

Good night, little cougar; you've had a hard day.

You injured your paw while you were at play.

But God heals our hurts and watches our ways.

Good night, little cougar; you've had a hard day.

Good night, little porcupine, high in a tree.

Are you hiding from God? Do you think He can't see?

If your heart is locked tight, He still has the key.

Good night, little porcupine, high in a tree.

Good night, little mouse; you're the smallest one here.

But with God on your side, you don't need to fear.

Every prayer that you tell Him, I know He will hear.

Good night, little mouse; you're the smallest one here.

Good night, little one in bed for the night.

I'll give you big kisses and hug you so tight

and remind you of how much God loves you tonight.

Good night, little one…I love you…good night.